STEP-BY-STEP EXPERIMENTS WITH ELECTRICITY

By Gina Hagler

Illustrated by Bob Ostrom

The Child's World®

Published by The Child's World®
1980 Lookout Drive • Mankato, MN 56003-1705
800-599-READ • www.childsworld.com

ACKNOWLEDGMENTS
The Child's World®: Mary Berendes, Publishing Director
The Design Lab: Design and production
Red Line Editorial: Editorial direction
Consultant: Dr. Peter Barnes, Assistant Scientist, Astronomy Dept.,
   University of Florida

ISBN 9781609733384
LCCN 2011940140

PHOTO CREDITS
Big Pants Production/Shutterstock Images, cover; Pilar Echeverria/
Dreamstime, cover, back cover; Murat Giray Kaya/iStockphoto, 1, 10,
29; Chris Twine/Shutterstock Images, 4; Shutterstock Images, 8, 20, 24;
Synchronista/Dreamstime, 14; M. Unal Ozmen/Shutterstock Images, 15;
Sergej Razvodovskij/Shutterstock Images, 25, 28

Design elements: Robisklp/Dreamstime, Pilar Echeverria/Dreamstime,
Sarit Saliman/Dreamstime, Jeffrey Van Daele/Dreamstime

Printed in the United States of America

BE SAFE !

The experiments in this book are meant for kids to do themselves. Sometimes an adult's help is needed though. Look in the supply list for each experiment. It will list if an adult is needed. Also, some supplies will need to be bought by an adult.

TABLE OF CONTENTS

What happens when you use a light switch?

CHAPTER ONE

Study Electricity!

What makes a light come on in your house? You turn on a switch. Then a lightbulb glows with light. But what makes the light glow? The switch lets **electricity** flow. It connects with the lightbulb. Electricity powers many things you use. It is a very important tool. We use it to keep our food cool and to see at night. It runs a radio so we can listen to music. And it keeps your computer on!

Electricity is a type of energy. It is made at a power plant. An electric **current** moves inside wires. The wires bring electricity to your home. A **battery** also makes electricity. Batteries let you bring electricity outside of your house. How can you learn more about electricity?

CHAPTER TWO

Seven Science Steps

Doing a science **experiment** is a fun way to discover new facts.
An experiment follows steps to find answers to science questions.
This book has experiments to help you learn about electricity.
You will follow the same seven steps in each experiment:

Seven Steps

1. Research: Figure out the facts before you get started.

2. Question: What do you want to learn?

3. Guess: Make a **prediction**. What do you think will happen in the experiment?

4. Gather: Find the supplies you need for your experiment.

5. Experiment: Follow the directions.

6. Review: Look at the results of the experiment.

7. Conclusion: The experiment is done. Now it is time to reach a **conclusion**. Was your prediction right?

Are you ready to become a scientist? Let's experiment to learn about electricity!

8

An electrician fixes and tests a circuit.

CHAPTER THREE

Complete a Circuit

What is inside machines? Most have a circuit. Learn how you can make a simple circuit.

Research the Facts

Here are a few. What else do you know?

- Electricity can flow through wires.
- Batteries make electricity.

Ask Questions

- What makes an electric circuit?
- How does a lightbulb turn on?

Make a Prediction

Here are two examples:

- The circuit will not light up the lightbulb.
- The circuit will light up the lightbulb.

Gather Your Supplies!

- Adult help
- A 9-volt battery
- 5 3-inch (8 cm) metal twist ties
- Lightbulb
- Bulb socket with screws (found at hardware or hobby stores)
- Pencil or pen
- Paper

Time to Experiment!

1. Remove the paper at the ends of the twist ties.
2. Screw the lightbulb into the socket.
3. Twist the ends of two 3-inch (8 cm) twist ties together. Do this again with two other twist ties. This makes two 6-inch (16 cm) twist ties. Be sure the paper is off the parts of the wire that touch!

4. Wrap one end of a long twist tie on a battery pole. The poles stick up on the end of the battery.

Battery Pole

5. Twist the short twist tie around a screw on the socket. Ask an adult for help. Make sure no paper from the twist tie touches the screw.

6. Twist the other end of the short twist tie to the other battery pole.

Twist tie wire

7. Twist the other long twist tie to the lightbulb. Make sure it is on the other screw of the socket.

8. Touch the two loose ends of the twist tie wires together. Do not let any paper touch the wires.

9. What happens to the lightbulb? Record what you see.

10. Pull apart the two loose ends of the twist tie wires.

11. What happens to the lightbulb? Record what you see.

Review the Results

Read your notes. What did the lightbulb do? When the wires touched, the lightbulb lit up. The lightbulb did not light up when the wires did not touch.

What Is Your Conclusion?

The wires and the battery made a circuit. When the wires did not touch, there was no circuit. An electric circuit needs a loop of wire and a power source. The power source was the battery. Power moved through the wires. The lightbulb turned on.

A light switch completes or breaks a circuit. That is why the light turns on and off.

CHAPTER FOUR

Can It Conduct?

Some things make circuits work.
A **conductor** lets electricity flow through it.
Other things are not good for circuits. An
insulator does not let electricity flow. See what
kinds of things are good conductors or insulators.

Research the Facts

Here are a few. What else do you know?

- A conductor completes a circuit.
- An insulator breaks a circuit.

Ask Questions

- What kinds of things are good conductors?
- What kinds of things are good insulators?

Does a wood spoon conduct electricity?

15

Make a Prediction

Here are two examples:

- Wood and plastic make good conductors.
- Wood and plastic make good insulators.

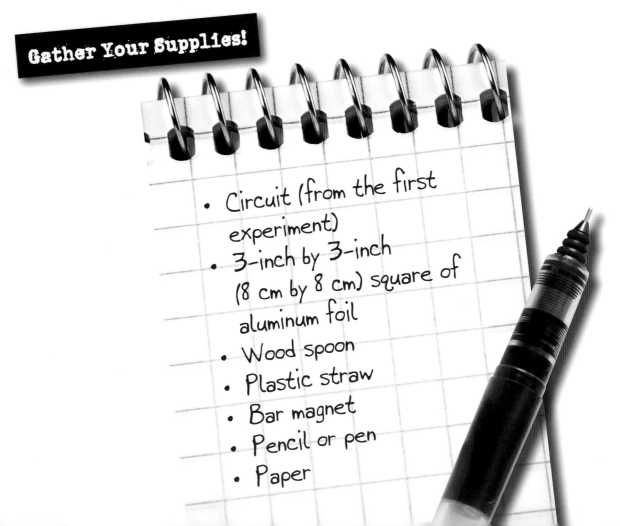

Gather Your Supplies!

- Circuit (from the first experiment)
- 3-inch by 3-inch (8 cm by 8 cm) square of aluminum foil
- Wood spoon
- Plastic straw
- Bar magnet
- Pencil or pen
- Paper

Time to Experiment!

1. Take the loose ends of the twist tie wires from the circuit. Touch them to the aluminum foil. Be careful not to touch the wires to each other.

2. Watch what happens to the lightbulb. Record what you see.

3. Take the loose ends of the wires again. Touch them to the wood spoon. What happens to the lightbulb? Record what you see.

4. Touch the loose ends of the wires to the plastic straw. Did the lightbulb turn on? Record what you see.

5. Now touch the wires to the bar magnet. What happens to the lightbulb? Record what you see.

Review the Results

Read your notes. Did the lightbulb turn on or stay off? It lit when the wires touched the aluminum foil and magnet. It did not light when the wires touched the wood spoon and the plastic straw.

What Is Your Conclusion?

Aluminum foil and magnets complete a circuit. They are both made of metal. Metal is a conductor. Wood and plastic break a circuit. They do not contain any metal. Wood and plastic are insulators.

Copper, silver, and gold are metals.
They all make great conductors.

Can balloons make static electricity?

CHAPTER FIVE

Electric Hair!

Have you felt a shock when you touched someone's hand? It is because of static electricity. See if you can make static electricity.

Research the Facts

Here are a few. What else do you know?

- Everything in the world is made of small parts called **atoms**.
- **Electrons** are parts of atoms.
- Electrons can move from one thing to another.

Ask Questions

- Do electrons move from a balloon to a person?
- How is static made?

Make a Prediction

Here are two examples:

- Static will come from a balloon and your hair.
- Static will not come from a balloon and your hair.

Gather Your Supplies!

- A balloon filled with air
- A room with a mirror
- Pencil or pen
- Paper

Time to Experiment!

1. Stand in front of the mirror. Make sure the light is on.
2. Rub the balloon back and forth on your hair.
3. Move the balloon away from your hair. Record what you see.
4. Turn off the light. Stand in front of the mirror.

In winter, the air is dry. Dry air helps this experiment work better.

5. Rub the balloon back and forth on your hair.

6. Slowly move the balloon away. Record what you see.

Review the Results

Look at your notes. Was static made? Your hair rose from your head. It moved when the balloon moved away. In the dark, you could see sparks when you moved the balloon.

What Is Your Conclusion?

Static electricity was made when the balloon rubbed on your hair. Electrons moved from the balloon to your hair. The balloon and your hair pulled to each other. You could see the electricity in the dark. It made sparks.

Static electricity makes your hair rise.

Static electricity cannot be stored in a battery. It also cannot be used to light our houses.

CHAPTER SIX

Lemon Battery

Batteries make electric energy. You use them in radios and toys. Learn how you can make a battery.

Research the Facts

Here are a few. What else do you know?

- Batteries have metal and an acid.
- Electrons move through battery acid.
- An electric current is the flow of electrons.

Ask Questions

- Where do electrons come from in a battery?
- Does acid help electrons move?

Make a Prediction

Here are two examples:

- Electrons will move in the lemon.
- Electrons will not move in the lemon.

25

Can a lemon become a battery?

Gather Your Supplies!

- Adult help
- Lemon
- Steel wool
- A copper nail
- A galvanized nail
- A sink
- Pencil or pen
- Paper

Time to Experiment!

1. Touch your tongue to the lemon. What do you feel? Write it down in your notes.

2. Scrub the nails with steel wool. Ask an adult for help. Make sure the nails are clean. Then rinse the nails in water.

3. Touch each clean nail head to your tongue. Do you feel anything? Write it down in your notes.
4. Ask an adult for help. Push the nails into the lemon. Put the nails 1 inch (2.5 cm) apart. Do not let the nails touch inside the lemon. The top of each nail should stick out. The points should be inside the lemon.
5. Stick out your tongue. Touch it to both nails at the same time.
6. What do you feel? Write it down in your notes.

Review the Results

Read your notes. You did not feel anything when your tongue touched only the lemon. You did not feel anything when your tongue just touched the nails. Your tongue tingled when it touched both nails in the lemon.

What Is Your Conclusion?

The lemon "battery" made electricity. Electrons moved from the nails. The electrons moved through the lemon. The nails were like metal in a battery. The lemon juice was like acid in a battery. You could feel the electricity when your tongue tingled.

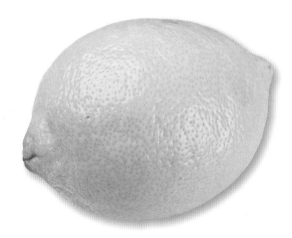

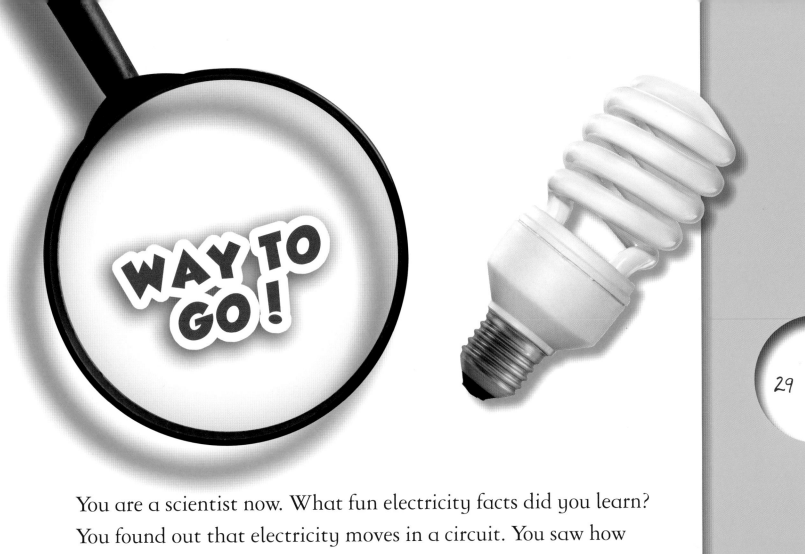

You are a scientist now. What fun electricity facts did you learn? You found out that electricity moves in a circuit. You saw how static electricity is made when electrons move from one object to another. You can learn even more about electricity. Study it. Experiment with it. Then share what you learn about electricity.

Glossary

atoms (AT-uhmz): Atoms are the smallest parts of something. Electrons are parts of atoms.

battery (BAT-uh-ree): A battery is a container that has metal and an acid and makes electricity. A battery makes electricity.

circuit (SUR-kit): A circuit is the complete path that electricity flows through. A light switch makes a circuit connect or break.

conclusion (kuhn-KLOO-shuhn): A conclusion is what you learn from doing an experiment. Her conclusion is that the wires can conduct electricity.

conductor (kuhn-DUHK-tur): A conductor is something that lets electricity flow through it. Metal is a good conductor.

current (KUR-uhnt): A current is the flow of electricity through a wire. A current flows through a circuit.

electricity (i-lek-TRISS-uh-tee): Electricity is a form of energy. We use electricity to make lightbulbs glow.

electrons (i-LEK-tronz): Electrons are tiny parts of atoms. Electrons can jump from one atom to another.

experiment (ek-SPER-uh-ment): An experiment is a test or way to study something to learn facts. This experiment showed the class how a circuit works.

insulator (IN-suh-late-or): An insulator is something that does not let electricity flow through it. Wood is an insulator.

prediction (pri-DIKT-shun): A prediction is what you think will happen in the future. His prediction that the balloon does not make static electricity was wrong.

socket (SOK-it): A socket is a hole where something fits in, such as a lightbulb. A lightbulb screws into a socket.

static electricity (STAT-ik i-lek-TRISS-uh-tee): Static electricity builds up on objects and is made when one object rubs against another. We can feel shocks from static electricity.

Books

Gray, Susan H. *Experiments with Electricity*. New York: Children's Press, 2012.

Lockwood, Sophie. *Super Cool Science Experiments: Electricity*. Ann Arbor, MI: Cherry Lake, 2010.

Mahaney, Ian F. *Electricity*. New York: PowerKids Press, 2007.

Web Sites

Visit our Web site for links about electricity experiments:
childsworld.com/links

Note to Parents, Teachers, and Librarians: We routinely verify our Web links to make sure they are safe and active sites. So encourage your readers to check them out!

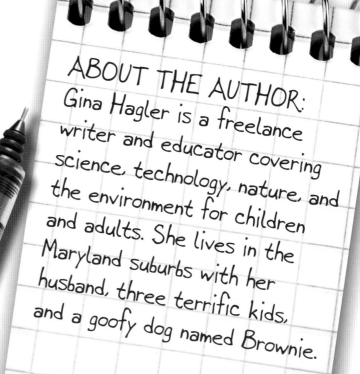

ABOUT THE AUTHOR:
Gina Hagler is a freelance writer and educator covering science, technology, nature, and the environment for children and adults. She lives in the Maryland suburbs with her husband, three terrific kids, and a goofy dog named Brownie.